Samassi

Published by
Adonis & Abbey Publishers Ltd
P.O. Box 43418
London
SE11 4XZ
http://www.adonis-abbey.com

First Edition, 31 March 2004

Copyright © Issaka K. Souare

British Library Cataloguing-in-Publication Data
A catalogue record for this book is available from the
British Library

ISBN 0-9545037-7-5

Cover Design   Ifeanyi Adibe

Printed and bound in Great Britain by Lightning
Source UK Ltd.

Samassi

By Issaka K. Souare

Other Books by Adonis & Abbey include:

Broken Dreams (Fiction/TCR1)
By Jideofor Adibe

Wooden Gongs and Drumbeats: African Folktales, Proverbs and Idioms (Fiction/TCR2) By Dahi Chris Onuchukwu

Nigeria and the Politics of Unreason: A study of the Obasanjo Regime (politics/political Economy)
By Victor E. Dike

The Making of the Africa-Nation: Pan Africanism and the African Renaissance (politics/political economy/political history)
Edited by Mammo Muchie

The Challenge of Authenticity: African Culture and Faith Commitment
By Jacob Hevi

Flight From Fate (Autobiography/sociology/Iroko Series 1)
By Evans Kinyua.

Dedication

To my grandparents, Madama and Siaka (Ndôma) Diabaté who loved me, cared for me and favoured me even over their own children, but passed away before I could do anything meaningful for them;

To my father, the late Kafoumba Souare who deceased before he could see me attempting to become what he always wanted me to be;

To my mother, Makagbe Diabaté, whose abiding love for me has helped me to overcome many challenges;

To my beloved wife, Aicha, whose love and moral comforting are a great source of strength for me;

To my friends: Baba M. Touré, Aboubacar AQ. Cissé and Moussa Doumbouya, for their genuine and unconditional support and encouragement;

To you... I dedicate this modest endeavour...

1

It was very cold in London that morning. Weather forecasters would describe it as freezing. The temperature was below zero. The snow had covered the old city with its beautiful white blanket. A seemingly violent but very cold wind was blowing every now and again. But, when they arrived at Gatwick airport, to the south of London, that Monday morning, Samassi and his friends did not feel the winter's cold until about five hours later.

Because they were six students – four young men and two girls – the cultural attaché sent by the embassy to pick them up couldn't come with his car. His blue BMW luxury car couldn't comfortably take more than four people. Nor could he have brought the embassy's white van that was meant to be used for such purposes. The van had been sent by the ambassador, two days earlier, for some personal businesses of his, somewhere in the countryside. Thus, Mr. Robert was driven by his chauffeur to

Victoria station, in central London, where he would board a fast train to the airport.

It was Sunday morning. His family – wife, son and two daughters had returned over the weekend from the United States, where they had spent their holidays. His family and their big screen hyper satellite television, with its over eighty channels, had kept him indoors, making him a real prisoner in the house over the weekend.

After about twenty minutes of waiting for the train at Victoria, the fast "Virgin" train on platform 17 was announced to be ready for boarding. The speaker nevertheless didn't forget to apologise to the commuters for the delay. Train timetables had been affected by the strong winds of last night. Trees had fallen on the rail track because of the blizzard. The Friday snow was now melting down. Instead of the usual half an hour between Victoria and Gatwick airport, Mr. Robert and his co-travellers spent three times as much time on that journey.

At the airport, Samassi accepted the delay. In fact, had it been his choice, he would have extended the delay a bit longer. The 24-year-old spent the time thinking and reflecting. He was so engrossed in his thoughts that he was, for the most part, oblivious of the presence of colleagues and their banters.

The young man was impressed by the loyal commitment of the Europeans to their pan-regional initiatives. At the customs and passport checkpoints, he found himself, with his colleagues, standing in an endless queue that kept extending itself as scores of new travellers joined it almost every five minutes. However, when he looked further down, on his right, he saw something different. He noticed a queue not quite like theirs. It was moving faster even though it had a bigger flow of people feeding it than theirs.

To add to his confusion, he saw some black people in that queue – as many blacks as there were whites on his own queue. He didn't understand why. He was still trying to fathom this out when he looked up and saw, atop the counter in that queue, and written in bold capital letters: **"EEC NATIONALS"**.

He had read extensively about the European integration project. He was impressed by their initiative on the free movement of peoples and goods within the zone. He remembered a similar initiative from his own West African region – the ECOWAS, and wondered why it appeared not to have been similarly implemented.

In the other queue, people didn't necessarily have to show their passports. Some presented to the customs officer what seemed to him to be mere ID cards. He had travelled on his passport within the West African sub-region, and he knew what he encountered during those journeys.

This wasn't the only thing that impressed the young Samassi. The technology, too, was seductive. He had always held the belief that humans were equal, regardless of their colour or race. But now, at the airport, the young man was faced with a challenge - how to reconcile his strong egalitarian beliefs with what he was witnessing.

This challenge grew bigger as they headed for central London, where they were to visit the embassy before being taken to their hostels. As they journeyed on, the six students got more and more excited. But Samassi not did allow himself to be over excited. Throughout, he kept on swamping the embassy's representative with questions. He had asked too many questions. Far too many to the point of irritating some of his colleagues.

The ambassador was not in. He was probably delayed by the bad weather. They decided to wait. At about 3pm, Mr. Robert called his Personal Assistant (PA) - ostensibly on a matter that was "confidential". He wanted to know what the PA had overheard the students saying amongst themselves. He was particularly interested in what Samassi might have said. But the PA said he could not remember anything about the boy in the grey jacket and black jeans:

"Look Dabo," said Mr. Robert to his PA, "we're in big trouble, you know."

"What do you mean, sir?" asked the PA quite confused. "Oh, do you mean that we cannot go to that lady's today because of the bad weather or probably because of the presence of these students and His Excellency hasn't come yet?"

"Come on Dabo! Why can't you understand such simple facts? It's true that the trouble is caused by the presence of the boys, but it hasn't got anything to do with that ugly lady."

"Eh, ugly lady, sir?" wondered the PA in a disapproving voice.

"Look, we're not there now. Listen, we're in a serious problem with these boys...their accommodation!"

"And what is wrong with that, sir? I think there is a budget for that. I could help find one foyer that could accommodate all of them at once."

"Do lower your voice a bit, please. Listen, you know you're my most trusted person in this embassy, don't you? The problem is... there is a budget actually. But, you know, emm...I mean...you know my family has just come back from holidaying in the States."

"Oh yes. But..."

"No, I mean...you see...Before they left for the holidays, things were not quite rosy with me, you know. The budget for the maintenance of those boys was approved and the money released to us at about this time." The PA was listening with blank expression as he had always done. Mr Roberts continued, lowering his voice now to the level of a whisper:

"I agreed with His Excellency ... well... to solve some of those personal problems from the fund. His Excellency unfortunately was in the same circumstances. We were sure we could refund whatever was taken by this time." He paused for any comment from the PA. He said nothing. "Of course a cabinet reshuffle could have taken care of this mess now", Mr Robert said, more to himself.

"Right, I see. But, if I can clearly understand this, there is still a portion of the money intact, sir?"
"Well, I'm not sure about that."

2

Save Maymouna and Adam, they had all learned English to some degree. Back home, Maymouna, at secondary school, had opted for Arabic as her foreign language. Adam, because of his elder brother, a Cuban-trained medical doctor, opted for Spanish. Samassi was much better in English than all his colleagues. He was also very proficient in Arabic and had even tried learning Russian. Only Ibrahim, who also spoke German, was more proficient in international languages than him.

In order to identify their respective appropriate levels, the procedure at the London College of English, in Fulham, southwest London, was to give all new candidates a "placement test". Samassi was admitted to "pre-intermediate" level, the fourth level at the school. Maymouna and Adam naturally sat in the "elementary" class, whilst the other three students had their seats in two different classes between the aforementioned two.

As far as lodging was concerned, they were dispersed over three different places. Maymouna and Sara got one shared room at a girls-only hostel in Shepherd's Bush, a few minutes' walk from the headquarters of BBC Television in west London. Etienne, Adam and Samassi shared one room in a privately rented residence in the Clapham Junction area. But Samassi would soon move, or rather be forced to move out to Camberwell Green, in southeast London. Ibrahim stayed with one of his friends in Putney, just a few minutes from the school.

Early in their studies, the six compatriots met regularly in the college's "common room", almost every break time. There, they would watch TV, play table tennis or engage in discussions with friends from other countries. However, as they gained more confidence in themselves and made friends from other countries, they began to spend days without seeing one another.

Samassi struck a friendship with a young man of about his age from South Korea. Kim Nung-nam had been offered a "conditional admission" for an MSc in Applied Microbiology at the prestigious Imperial College in London. The "condition" was that he must improve his English and have IELTS (International English Language Testing System) with at least 6.5 as the overall mark. Kim was attending English language courses at post-intermediate level.

They first met in the "listening room" on the ground floor of the school. Some three weeks later, they had become very close friends.

Kim, like Samassi, had a scholarship from his country. But, there was a mountain-size difference between the conditions of the two. Whilst Samassi shared a single room with two other mates, had very modest meals, and hardly went out, Kim, on the other hand, shared a three bedroom flat with just two colleagues. They ate delicious food from their country and had liberal access to the good things of life. When they didn't cook at home or didn't want to, they could pop in to an Italian restaurant for a meal of pasta, or to an Indian one for a large take-away portion of sliced chicken with rice. And while Samassi lived in zone two in the Clapham Junction area, Kim had his flat in Kensington, one of London's more exclusive areas.

On the face of it, this difference could be due to the economic disparity between their two countries. On a closer examination however, one could see there was more to it.

Just four months into their stay in London, the young Samassi, together with Ibrahim, got invited to the embassy. At first, he was very excited about the invitation. He thought that the officials at the embassy might have considered the suggestions they had sent to them. They had requested the amelioration of their conditions. The landlady had warned them that they would be evicted if they did not pay up their outstanding rents.

He had got confused when Ibrahim told him that he, too, had received a similar letter from the embassy. Ibrahim never took part in writing the SOS letter to the embassy. He never depended much on the embassy.

Alone, Samassi spent time reflecting on the invitation. He was more perplexed that the invitation was on a day that his mid term exam would start. He had stated such clearly in his SOS letter to the embassy. After days of thinking this over, he called the embassy for clarification. Mr Robert was blunt that keeping that Wednesday appointment was more important than "his exam issue at the school".

On Wednesday, at 10:30am, Samassi and Ibrahim were ushered into Mr. Robert's office by his Personal Assistant. They observed that the cultural attaché did not look as healthy as he looked the last time they saw him.

"Make yourselves comfortable", Mr Robert said, trying to appear friendly. Just then the phone rang. He appeared listless, then panicked. He mumbled a few incoherent sentences – apparently in answer to questions from the voice on the other line. Suddenly he became conscious of their presence and motioned them to wait outside his office. It was not until two hours later that Samassi and Ibrahim heard again from Mr Roberts. It was delivered through Mr Dabo, his PA. The message was terse: Their scholarship was to be suspended at the end of the month because of budgetary constraints. The Deputy Director of the Department of Foreign Scholarships at the Ministry of Higher Education and Research signed the letter.

As Mr Dabo, a Sierra Leonian delivered the message and the letter, his expression was forlorn, and there was a certain frown of disapproval on the left side of his lower lip. He had not been paid for three months and was really getting irritated by all the 'monkey business' going on in the embassy.

***

Mr Roberts emerged from his office to expatiate on the letter just as Samassi and Ibrahim were about to leave. He lowered his voice, and in a suppressed fury that was obviously contrived, complained about the politicians back home not having a clue of the kind of hardship foreign students faced in Europe. He hissed in sympathy and invited Ibrahim and Samassi back to his office.

After making sure the office was closed, he told them, in a hushed tone, that he was on their side, and that what they needed to do was to think clearly, and rationally consider their options.

"You boys could be my children. Well, my first son is now 20, almost in the same age group as you. You may have heard that he is studying in Canada. It's very sad to see one's ultimate ambitions being obstructed like this." He paused to gauge the reactions of the two students.

They said nothing, too lost in their own thoughts.

He continued: "The letter from the Department has given you two options. I don't know whether you would be able to support yourselves and thus stay on until perhaps next year. But, placing myself in the position of your parents and in the spirit of carrying out a patriotic duty, I could somehow help you. Because you're still learning English and have shown good progress, especially you Samassi, I am ready to personally bear the costs of two of you continuing your English language studies in Africa, preferably in Nairobi Kenya, where I have a friend who could look after you."

He paused again. The two students looked bemused.

3

It was a very sad evening for Samassi. He had always dreamed of studying in England. Now he was seeing the flame of his ambitions flickering.

He agreed to go home with Ibrahim, where the latter lived with his friend in Putney. On their way, they kept analysing the situation and weighing their options. They were utterly confused.

Boubacar, Ibrahim's friend and host, had just come back from work when they got home. He had not met Samassi before, but he had heard of him many times. He greeted them cheerfully and warmly. From their countenances he suspected there was something fishy. Boubacar was not as moved as they expected him to be after they had narrated the incident at the embassy earlier in the day. He gave an ironic smile. "You two are attaching undue importance to these degrees. They are just papers you know, and not necessarily a condition for success in life."

Samassi and his friend were bemused.

"I mean, you're only looking for these papers, degrees or certificates or whatever you call them. Then after you have got them, what? Will you become ministers immediately afterwards? Life is always full of rich alternatives. When one door closes another one usually opens. But you have to be strong when one door is closing to be able to see the opening one"

Samassi and his friend remained bemused.

Boubacar continued. "From what you have said I think this man may genuinely want to help you through your English language classes in Kenya. A part of me however is not convinced. But even if he does help, what happens after the language course in Kenya?"

A long minute of silence snaked by. From where they were, they could hear Boubacar singing in the kitchen and shuffling his feet in obvious imitation of his favourite rock singer.

Ibrahim was familiar with this kind of advice. It was four months into their stay in London, and over this period, Boubacar wouldn't miss a single opportunity advice to his childhood friend.

Ibrahim turned to his friend Samassi with these words: "I'm very sad about the situation. But, I think that everything will be fine in the end. Here we have the three options from the cultural attaché. Then there is the advice from my friend, Bouba. I think this is the first time you are meeting with him. Perhaps I need to tell you a bit about him and our friendship. But, I don't know, what do you think about his advice?

Samassi merely lifted up his head and said nothing.

By the time he left, Samassi was very convinced that he was going to be a "one-man army" in the struggle. Although the night had spread its cover on the city, he decided to pop into Kim's in Kensington. From the outset, his Korean friend advised him to opt for the Nairobi option. And if he didn't want that, Kim observed, he would then advise him to return to his home country. Samassi was not enthused by the idea. He never found the going-home option an attractive proposition. He knew what fate awaited him there. The Kenyan option was also not attractive to him precisely for the same fear that it would all end up to his having to return to his home country. "Not now!" he muttered to himself resolutely.

He came back home that day quite late. It was unusual for him and that got his mates, Etienne and Adam, worried. When the two young women, Sara and Maymouna, heard the news, Sara favoured the Kenyan option. Etienne suggested they should sleep over the options and not rush into a decision. Maymouna opined that they should contact their parents back home to verify the authenticity and accuracy of the cultural attaché's claims. She had strong reasons for doubting the integrity of Mr. Robert.

4

Maymouna was a pretty young lady. This was reflected in the fact that she was named Diallo. Majority of the "Diallos" belong to the Fula ethnic group, believed to be among the prettiest people in West Africa, if not in the whole of Africa. She was terrifically charming and extremely attractive. And how does a man without scruples like Mr. Robert relate to such an attractive young lady? He had always assumed that as the cultural attaché, he was the students' guardian and the person to look after them in the UK.

From the very moment he saw her at Gatwick airport, a sudden but powerful emotional spark had been ignited his heart. He felt very strongly attracted to the young woman. A month later, he found an excuse to invite her to his office. He deliberately chose a Saturday morning for the invitation. When the young lady wondered why she should be summoned on a Saturday when the embassy was supposed to be officially closed, he claimed he had a huge workload with tight deadlines, and that the ambassador had asked him to work weekends to clear the backlog of cases on his desk.

She had her doubts but decided to honour the invitation any way.

Alone in the office, Mr. Robert talked non-stop, flirtatiously, even a little boastfully in a bid to impress her. It was as if he was drunk, disclosing what he might under different circumstances never have done. He revealed things that common sense would have counselled otherwise. Finally, he mustered the courage to lay the cards on the table. "To be honest, my darling, since I saw you, I mean from the very first day I saw you, I have had strong feelings for you." He paused to gauge her reaction. She said nothing. Her expression was blank.

"You know, it takes a while and a deep analysis from someone like me to trust such feelings and temptations. But I think my feelings for you are genuine and strong."

Maymouna ignored his words and tried to change the subject. When Mr Robert persisted on the subject in a bid to get her to discuss it, she strongly expressed her disapproval – by her body language and expressions. He got the message and felt embarrassed.

Sensing his weakness, she said she had a big favour to ask.

"Go on. I am here to help. I help many on a daily basis".

She crossed her legs, such that the slit on the sides of her blue skirt briefly displayed her succulent laps. He swallowed hard.

"You are very beautiful", he said, his mind reflecting on the laps it saw and where it led. "I am worried about my brother back home. I would want him to get good quality education".

He sensed the request that was to follow and regretted the timing, saying that had the request come three days earlier, he would have been in a position to do something. "I could even have helped him to come and be with you here in the UK."

"Could you do that?"

"Well, I know what I'm talking about. Perhaps you don't know me well."

"But, we could negotiate it, darling, couldn't we?" she said, gently caressing his cheeks with the soft palm of her hand and a teasing smile.

He felt the softness of the touch and something began raising its head in his underpants. He held her hands in his and stared longingly at her.

"Don't worry. I'll see what I can do for you. Just give me his details. I could ask my friend to insert his name somewhere in the next group of students who will be offered scholarship to France. But, you'll be responsible for his travel fares and living costs for the first three months before things get sorted out."

"Waoo! I'll highly appreciate that…"

"Trust me," he said with a roguish smile.

"Of course I trust you. I know you can do it", she said flirtatiously.

He held her left hand and squeezed it gently.

"I can't thank you enough".

"Oh, never mind. It's nothing."

"But how are you going to do it?" she asked suddenly. "Are you going to add his name to an existing list or substituting his name for another name in the list?"

She suspected it would be the latter scenario whereby another student would be deprived of his or her right for her brother.

By the time she left the embassy that day, she had learnt a lot - not just about how the embassy was run but about how bursaries and scholarships were given and denied. She also learnt that Mr Roberts and the ambassador were very close friends, and they had some common business interests, which he said he could not disclose to anyone. He also let her know that he had a web of strong contacts back home, at both the Ministry of Foreign Affairs and that of Higher Education and Research.

The meeting with Mr Roberts that Saturday informed her suggestion that Samassi and his friend, Ibrahim, should first verify the authenticity of the story from Mr Roberts. She had always been Samassi's secret admirer.

As they were still unable to get any correct assessment of the situation from home by Saturday, she suggested that Samassi should choose to stay behind and struggle to support himself. "God will help", she said. She couldn't intervene, as she wasn't at that particular moment on good terms with Mr. Robert.

This was in any case what Samassi had already made up his mind to do. On Sunday evening, at her request, Samassi and Maymouna met in a modest Caribbean restaurant near their hostel in Shepherd's Bush. Maymouna had thought of the web of contacts that Mr. Robert boasted about when they met in his office three months earlier. She thought that with such contacts back home, if her friend was a victim of a fraudulent manoeuvre, as she felt convinced he was, then it would be difficult for them to get to the truth, for as the saying goes, "one never finds the needle that is knowingly under the foot of one of your co-searchers".

5

Mondays always seemed to have special significance for Samassi. Though a few of the significant occurrences for him on Mondays could be considered good or beneficial, for the most part, Mondays always carried sad news for him. It was on a Monday that he lost his father some eleven years back. It was also on a hot Monday afternoon that he found himself in a police van, accused of masterminding a major student demonstration that, according to the authorities, incited people to revolt against the government. He spent 121 days in jail without trial – despite the fact that he was innocent of the accusation. It was also on a Monday that Mr Roberts dropped his bombshell.

Samassi was able to secure a temporary accommodation before the 10-day deadline given by the cultural attaché for him to leave the room on Cowrie Street elapsed. His two roommates, Etienne and Adam jointly offered him £215 as support.

Maymouna, Sara and his Korean friend, Kim, helped too.

He moved into a student hostel in Camberwell Green, in South-East London. There, he shared a room with three other students from different countries. The four roommates were a real multicultural mix. Samassi was an African, Raj was originally from Nepal but based in India, Abdurrahman was from Malaysia, and Andrew was from Poland.

Raj was very proud of India. He somehow had family links to Mahatma Ghandi. Samassi had observed that he was never the type to rush into judgements or hasty actions. A good listener, he admired the economic and technological achievements of the West but had reservations about their social values.

Abdurrahman was a very patient guy. He hardly got upset. A devout Muslim, he was very sociable and open to all his colleagues regardless of their religious beliefs. If one didn't know him, one would think that he was constantly preparing for one exam or the other. Though he was studying for an IT qualification, he was often seen reading non-IT books such as books on development studies, politics, biographies, international relations, international political economy and the history of Western countries. Despite working extremely hard, Abdu, as he was fondly called, never believed he worked hard enough. Abdu also liked to talk about his country, Malaysia, especially its policy of "Looking Eastwards", which encouraged Malaysians to learn from the experiences of Japan and other Asian 'tigers'.

Samassi considered Andrew, the Polish fellow, a nice guy, but didn't believe he knew him well enough.

Samassi's cost of living skyrocketed as soon as he moved out of Cowrie Street. As opposed to before, when he and his roommates shared the cooking and costs, he now found himself doing his own cooking. He found this not only more expensive but also more time-consuming. Because he now lived further away from his school, his transportation cost also rose astronomically.

A few weeks into all these, fortune smiled on his colleagues- Etienne, Adam, Sara and Maymouna. The British Council had allocated seven full scholarships to the government. But, instead of submitting seven new names, the government submitted the names of the four students 'now on their charge' and who were already in London, plus three others. Since the scholarships were never advertised, filling the remaining three slots became an interesting affair. Mr Roberts, as usual, was at the centre of many of the plots. Each slot was being offered for as high as $10,000.

Not long after Samassi moved to Camberwell Green, his roommates moved to live outside London, leaving him on his own. He knew he needed extra energy, courage, determination and hard work to survive. He had always believed in himself, and in fact saw his quest for further education as a deliberate preparation for eventually confronting some of the ills he saw and abhorred in his country. He believed that most of the ills in his country were also endemic in other countries and cultures. But he often wondered why those ills seemed more paralytic in his country than in many of the so-called developed world.

<u>6</u>

True, Maymouna was particularly beautiful. But compared to Regina, she would seem not to be all that. Only 20 years of age, she was well built, tall, elegant and charming.

Regina was a mixed-race - born to a black African father and a white German mother. Samassi first met her when she came from Germany to visit one of her friends living in a different wing of the students' hostel in Camberwell. He saw her during one of the cultural and social events usually organised on Friday evenings at the St Joseph's wing. He didn't take much notice of her then.

At the London College of English, students were entitled to a certain number of weeks of holiday based on their enrolment period. Whilst on holiday, other students would nevertheless continue their lessons. Upon the students' return from their holidays, they would join the class wherever they might be in the programme. And because students could attend classes on any Monday, provided there was a place at their appropriate level, it was very common for holidaymaking students to find many new faces in their classroom.

Back from a six-week holiday, most of which he spent working; Samassi was surprised to see in the class someone he was convinced he had seen before. He thought very hard. He was sure he had met her before. But where? He tried to catch her attention but couldn't. She was sitting in the far corner, apparently oblivious of what was going on in his mind- or of his existence for that matter.

She was wearing a short skirt and transparent shirt. That seemed to be the rage on that particularly hot summer day. It was not too long before he convinced himself that she was the same lady he had seen some two months back in the St. Joseph's wing of his hostel in Camberwell Green.

He remembered a difference between the lady he saw at St Joseph's wing and the one in his class. The one from St. Joseph's wing was energetic, dynamic, enthusiastic for questions and seemingly sociable. In contrast, the one in the class was a little withdrawn. During the break, she sat alone, reading a novel, while the other ladies, in their skimpy dresses and sunglasses, chatted noisily and flirtatiously.

Samassi observed her throughout the week, and made many fruitless efforts to establish eye contacts or conversations with her. When on the Friday, the class teacher, Miss Sophie, invited the class to a restaurant for launch, Samassai became expectant.

She sat alone while the others sat three-four to a table. Suddenly three African male students placed their foods on her table and went to the counter to buy some drinks. She took her book, bag and other belongings and left the table before the Africans returned to their foods. She found another empty table, and sat on one of the four chairs. Not long afterwards, three young white ladies joined her at the table. They were chatting happily and tried to be friendly to her. She felt conscious and did not talk much, her face buried in the novel she was reading – or pretended to be reading. From where he sat, Samassi observed all these with interest and curiosity.

Some two days later, his paths crossed hers. It was during a group discussion in their class.

"Hi, my name is Samassi. We were together at that restaurant on Friday", he said, putting on his charms.

"Oh", she said. She was not unfriendly but also not particularly excited.

"So where are you from exactly?" he asked, trying desperately to sustain her interest in the discussion.

"Germany. Why do you want to know?"

"Oh, curiosity."

She smiled a half-face smile.

"Is one of your parents African?"

She said nothing. It was obvious from her facial expression that she was not enthused by the question.

"So, you're German!" a Swedish young lady sitting next to them exclaimed.

"I said that I was from Germany and that's all you could know," she retorted.

Not long after this incidence, the teacher was discussing "multiculturalism" and wanted to know how the students would classify themselves. Samassi noted that she neither wanted to be identified as European nor as an African, claiming instead that she was a global citizen. Samassi was more puzzled.

One day he mustered enough courage and asked if he could talk to her in private. But she turned down the invitation. Samassi was hurt, not so much by the rejection, but by the way it was done. He felt she was utterly rude to him.

<u>7</u>

In school classrooms – whatever the level may be - students who are remarkably intelligent usually win others' hearts and minds. Both Samassi and Regina were remarkably brilliant students. Samassi represented the top of the gents and Regina the top of the ladies. True, they were not reading a specialist course. They were only learning English as a language. But their brilliance shone clearly.

Samassi was not only brilliant in class, he was also a good footballer and very sociable. In addition, he was a very patient but resolute fellow. Regina was gradually attracted to these qualities in Samassi. She still had her opinions of Africans – the usual stereotypes. But she gradually began to warm up to Samassi as she saw him as being different.

Samassi was unaware that she was beginning to warm up to him. He did notice on a few occasions that she appeared friendlier but he didn't want to read much meaning into that. He merely regarded it as one of those mood changes that could happen to anyone.

One day an opportunity presented itself. They began talking, first about their studies, then about books, London, and life in general. It was a warm, friendly discussion, in which both shared a common opinion on many of the issues they discussed.

As they talked and enjoyed the talk, Samassi wasn't sure if he should take the opportunity to ask her out. He wanted very much to do so. But at the same time he did not want to spoil things by being too eager and hasty. Suddenly both fell silent. The silence lasted for a long minute. Samassi tried to focus his gaze on her. She smiled, a friendly smile that warmed his veins.

"Its really been nice talking to you", Samassi finally said, in a voice tinged with longing and desire.

"It's been really nice talking to you, Samassi," she said. Mentioning his name once again sent certain thrills through his veins.

"It will be nice to meet again. May be for lunch."

"Why not?" he replied, even before she finished the sentence. They agreed to meet at Burgess Park in Camberwell.

At four o'clock in the afternoon, Samassi went to Burgess Park to meet his date. There were many people in the park that day. Some played football, some ran in the fields, and some just lay on their backs, sunbathing. In the park, many people were in pairs. Some appeared to be just interested in observing what others in the park are doing, while a handful – engaged themselves, under the trees here and there, in some romantic stuff better not described here.

She appeared about fifteen minutes later. She was wearing long sports trousers and a Nike jacket with a matching cap. She looked quite athletic in the outfit. "Oh, was it you over there? I did see you a little while ago but couldn't recognise you," Samassi said. She took that as a compliment and smiled.

"I am sorry for being a little late. I took a bus going in a completely different direction."

They both burst into laughter, with Samassi narrating incidents where he had made such mistakes himself.

She sat next to him on a bench. "So how are you coping with your course?"

"Oh, fine. And you?"

"Very fine. I think Sophie is a great teacher, isn't she?"

For the next twenty minutes, they talked about their course, and of virtually everyone in the class. Then they fell silent.

"Regina!" he began, looking her straight in the eyes and crossing his legs. "You're a very lovely girl. I mean you're very intelligent and ambitious. I'm very impressed by you. I greatly admire you."

He paused.

"Thank you. I think you are also a nice fellow."

"Thank you very much." He was pleased she regarded him as a nice fellow.

"I have difficulty in understanding you. I think others do, too", Samassi confessed. He told her he had been observing her in the class. "When you said you were from Germany, I was quite excited. And although my first thought was to somehow link you to an African origin, I quickly realised that people are and should be recognised to be from where they choose, as long as they are happy with that." He paused.

She said nothing.

"I was rather surprised the way you had reacted to questions of where you came from, and of whether one of your parents was black".

She apologised for her reaction but quickly added: "That is how I am, and I am sure if you knew my situation very well, you could find this normal."

"What do you mean?"

After a short pause, she replied with these words: "Samassi, to be quite honest with you, as an African, I don't quite trust you. But I had an irresistible urge from the deep inside of me to come to meet you here this evening..." She stood up, concealing her face from him. She didn't want him to see the tears in her eyes. But Samassi could sense what was happening.

"Regina, are you all right?" He was concerned. He moved closer to her. She was touched by his concern, which seemed genuine. They sat down, but on the grass this time round.

Regina began narrating her life history, of how she had never known her father. "I'm not an orphan. But I'm worse than orphans. I'm made to believe that I have a father who is still alive somehow somewhere in this world. But I don't know

47

where. I'm told he was from Africa. But I don't know from which country, nor am I certain about even his name."

Samassi was listening attentively.

"My mother tells me he was a 'crook'. He told her he was from Liberia but she later found out he wasn't from that country. He apologised and gave the name of another country, but it also turned out he wasn't from that country. My mum wasn't even sure he told her his real name."

That's not nice," Samassi said.

"My mother claims she came across three different names of him. She was deeply shocked when, one day she found a Congolese ID card bearing his photo with a name she had never known him for. She later found out that he wasn't from the Congo either!"

A very tall white lady in skimpy dress and sunglasses walked past where they were sitting. The much shorter man she was walking with was literally trying to dip his hands under her skirt. They cast quick glances at them and ignored them. She continued with her story.

"I was barely 18 months when he left. So, I didn't get to know him. But he left with everything that could allow me to one day trace him. Or at least, see my uncles, aunts. Perhaps my mother did it. Whenever she's angry, she always discharges her anger on me."

She stopped and smiled. It was a funny, dry smile meant at herself. It was obvious to Samassi that she was trying hard to suppress her emotions. He scratched his head and briefly looked away to avoid making eye contacts with her.
She continued.

"I'm not sure if she doesn't hate me. She seems sometimes to see me as my father rather than as me. And in the streets, I am faced with discrimination and racism"

She added, half-jokingly, but with a tinge of sadness: "I'm abandoned. I don't know where and to whom I belong. But what I still don't understand about my dad is why he got himself involved in fathering a child when he knew he wasn't going to be around that child."

Samassi quickly remembered his weekend trip with Kim, to France, about five months earlier. Many of the black people they had approached for directions to the Eiffel tower never even bothered to stop. Samassi had also observed the barely concealed antagonism between migrant black Africans and people from the Caribbean. He had thought such behaviour was a carry over from the colonial days, when those working for the colonial establishments or working for white men considered themselves superior to those not similarly 'blessed'. Regina's story now offered a new angle for the apparent animosity between many Europeans of mixed ancestry and their black African counterparts.

"I'm very sorry to hear this. It's very sad. I hope your father hasn't abandoned you forever. He might have been unable, for one reason or the other to do just what is right."

" For eighteen years?"

"I think you should also try to be positive with Africans. The regrettable failings of one individual are not enough to pigeonhole an entire race of people. I also don't buy the idea that European streets indiscriminately hate black people. True, racism and discrimination exist. However, there are a lot of decent people out there who don't club with racists. They just see and treat you the way you present yourself. You see what I mean."

8

They became close friends after the meeting at the Burgess Park. Everyone in the class was astonished. She had become livelier and no longer "that black German lady who never talks to anyone". Behind their backs, people gossiped and wondered what Samassi did to her, and what she saw in him. Some thought that they were lovers but they weren't. Their relationship and closeness were about something else.

Samassi had an ambition and a vision for his continent, Africa. He had a vision of Africa, free of sufferings, misery and backwardness.

For Regina, a mixed race girl deprived of a father's love; hers was a quest for identity. Although she wasn't very sure if her father actually came from Africa, she felt a certain link with the continent.

They got closer every day. It was such that if one looked at the 'dialled numbers' menu of Samassi's phone, Regina's number would always come in the last three numbers dialled. Likewise, if people were to be asked to pay for others' bills for calls made to them, Samassi would have certainly been liable for no less than ninety-five per cent of Regina's.

They talked a lot about their experiences in Europe, racism, opportunities, the situation in Africa and so forth. One day the discussion was on ethnic minorities and how the current state of Africa disadvantaged blacks in Europe and America. One of their friends, Yakubu, a Nigerian who liked to use big English words lectured them on the concept of 'ethnic minorities', which they were freely using in the discussion:

"Well, I think we should first remind ourselves of the legal definition of 'national minorities'. That is 'minority groups who have a king state' - that is, a state where their people originally come from. This means that 'national minorities' are those people who became so as a result of boundary changes or other factors, but still have the largest representation in their ancestors' land. And this is also true for you, Regina."

"Professor!" Samassi hailed him, jokingly and they all began laughing. Yakubu continued.

"This brings us to the link between these black people and Africa, as their 'king state'. Hence the nomenclature African-Americans, African-Brazilians, Afro-Europeans, etc. Thus, in my view, the image of Africa has an absolutely important role to play here. My argument is that throughout history, people are normally measured and often treated according to what others perceive of them in terms of the presence of protectors for them. For example, who would dare to maltreat an American or a British national today? How are Russians abroad treated today compared to just about few years ago?"

"Professor Yakubu!". Samassi knew Yakubu liked arguments. He gave him the nickname of *Professor.*

"Thus, if Africa had better economic, political and, perhaps, military conditions, Africans abroad and people like Regina would be treated better."

They agreed with Yakubu's analysis of the situation.

"It couldn't have been put better than this," Regina said.

"You're absolutely right," agreed Samassi and added: "...and this is where our responsibility as Africans lies. This is our job. I'm sure if we are able to better our lives back home, as Yakubu rightly suggested, that would make a huge difference. We have to work for it. No one else can do it but us..."

<u>9</u>

Often people with bona fide intentions for noble causes are not easily discouraged. The difficulties such people face in trying to realise their dreams could often be a test of their resolve and determination. And since the goal is noble, experiencing some difficulties could even benefit the person as it may increase the value of the object, and therefore the willingness to guard it jealously.

It was in this spirit that Samassi, despite the ups and downs he faced since his scholarship was withdrawn, managed eventually to enrol for a postgraduate degree in Development Studies. As a foreign student, he didn't have any choice but to go for the full time option.

During the course of his search for a university place, and for means of paying his tuition fees and other expenses, he had contacted as many universities as possible within the UK. All the prospectuses sent raised his hopes that he would secure some funding. The prospectuses were full of statistics of students who had been offered one scholarship or the other by one agency or NGO.

Reality dawned on him when, after securing a place in one of the universities, he began applying for these scholarships. He applied to so many that he virtually lost count. He eventually gave up, after his telephone bill had gone up to the roof – from making so many calls to too many agencies, who sometimes kept him on hold and forgot about him.

He applied to study part-time to enable him combine his studies with working to raise money for his tuition fees. He knew it wasn't going to be easy. But then he never really had anything on a platter of gold.

Before he formally began the programme, he had made sure that he had short-listed some specialist magazines and periodicals that he would be reading at the university's library. He had similarly short-listed some books, many of them outside the official curriculum. He was nearly always in the library that his fellow students nicknamed him, "Assistant

Librarian". Coincidentally he also later got a part-time job at the library.

One day Samassi found himself having a rather long discussion with the supervisor of the security guards in the library. He was a well-built, tall and handsome African, from Zambia. Though the man never seemed particularly enthusiastic about his job, he nonetheless was always polite and friendly to everyone coming to, or leaving the library.

As they talked, Samassi told him of some of the challenges he faced; the fact that he slept only two or three hours every day because he had to combine work with studies and his fruitless search for scholarship. Edward, the security supervisor, who was in his 50s, also told Samassi of some of his own problems.

He had married Takumba, a fellow Zambian. He married her, not because of her beauty, for he didn't think she was particularly beautiful. He married her because he thought her responsible. He had then been in England for three years and had visited Zambia specifically to marry. He was very particular he needed to know the family pedigree of anyone he married and had expressed preference for girls from his village or the neighbouring villages. That alone ruled out marrying any of the girls he had met in the UK.

He had in fact had a brief relationship with her before he left for England. When he returned to look for a wife, none of the girls he was introduced impressed him. He distrusted those who openly flirted with him and dropped hints of their willingness to marry. He wasn't sure if they merely wanted to use him to come to the UK or if they genuinely liked him, and could, with time, come to love him.

The first problem was bringing her over to live with him in the UK. He was doing minimum wage jobs and also had no permanent residence permit. But after many efforts, including borrowing money from friends, he eventually succeeded in bringing her over to the UK.

The marriage soon became turbulent and fell apart a few years later. It all started with a row over who would take their youngest child to the hospital. It was a bitter row but nothing physical. Two of Takumba's closest friends – both single mothers, were big influences on her, were constantly on the phone, ringing to her virtually every ten minutes. By the time

Edward came back from work, the lock to his apartment had been changed. Takumba had called the police, alleging that her husband had threatened her with a knife and had nearly strangled her in a brawl. Her two single-mother girlfriends were there and gave evidence. The police advised her to change the locks.

When he returned home and found himself unable to open the door, with some of his shirts and trousers in a Tesco polythene bag outside their door, a call suddenly came from the police on his mobile phone: He must not be seen within one mile of his home – or charges would be brought against him.

The following day, he went to withdraw money from their joint account, and found the account empty. He never kept a separate account. For weeks, he lived rough, sometimes squatting with friends who lived very far away from his work. He was distraught. He lost his job not long afterwards and also spent time in psychiatric wards.

The man's story was very touching. Samassi felt very sorry for him and showed genuine sympathy. Edward had now been divorced for four years. He said he worked just to be able to pay for child support; a sum he thought was arbitrarily fixed without taking into consideration his personal circumstances.

Samassi expressed concerns about the rate at which African marriages fell apart in the Western world, and wondered if that should not be discouraging to young men like him.

<u>10</u>

It was July, the end of the academic year. Samassi had handed in his dissertation. The graduation ceremony was to be in December at the prestigious Barbican Centre in central London.

Samassi wasn't worried about whether he would pass in flying colours. He knew he would. He was always top of his class in virtually every module.

He was thrilled that it had eventually come to an end, that he was on the verge of fulfilling his academic ambitions despite the odds. He believed the graduation would pave way for realising his broader dream. He must never let his dream of one day making a positive difference in the development of his country die.

Despite his joy, he was conscious of the fact that he was still struggling financially. A prize he had won in an essay competition had helped in paying part of his tuition fees. Yes, he worked part-time. But his income was insufficient to cater for his maintenance, books and paying off the remaining tuition fees. He had to borrow – sometimes from anyone willing to lend. So, yes, graduation was a joyous occasion. But it was also pay back time.

He had begun hunting for jobs as soon as he had handed in his dissertation. He couldn't rely on his part time Librarian Assistant job at the university anymore. The pay, given also the fact that it was part-time job, was a peanut. In any case, his eligibility for the job would expire by the end of August. He needed a *real job* – to pay off his debt, meet some of his obligations to relatives back in his home country. He also needed to gain the necessary professional experience for his future career plans. He needed, too, to work and save some money to enable him return and resettle in his home country.

He was never in doubt that he would get a *good* job. He was an enthusiastic reader of the jobs section of several newspapers and websites and was always impressed by what he saw as the array of opportunities available for new graduates. He felt confident he met the academic requirements for many of the adverts he read.

He was not unmindful of some of the hurdles before him. He knew he had to satisfy the legal requirements for a full work permit, not a student visa that only allowed him to work for a restricted number of hours. His student visa didn't legally allow him to take any full time employment beyond holiday or vacation periods. Besides, his student visa was to expire in the next few months. In theory, he could be offered a full time employment with the condition to change his immigration status. And that condition had to be met by him, although with the support of a potential employer. That would require the potential employer issuing him with a recommendation letter to the Home Office (the Interior Ministry) charged with the task of regulating immigration affairs in the country.

With this option in mind he felt quite positive and began applying to as many jobs as he could. He also put on his details on many of the free online job search databases.

It didn't take too long for it to dawn on him that he had perhaps been too optimistic. He had applied for well over one hundred jobs between July and February.

Some of the jobs he applied for were in fact outside London. Some two-thirds never bothered to even acknowledge the receipt of his application. The remaining one-third had different ways of telling him the same story – crudely put, that they were not going to offer him the job. All the replies were unfailingly polite and each wished him "good luck" in his job hunt.

A few invited him for an interview. He was elated when he received the first letter inviting him for an interview. He believed his prayers had been answered. He danced around his room in excitement and phoned his friend Alex to tell him that the boat was approaching the shores.

All the five interviews he attended had the same outcome. Those who interviewed him were exceptionally friendly, and at the end of the interview, promised to send him a letter or phone him to let him know of their decision.

He didn't hear from them for a long time after the interview. When eventually the letters came, there were different explanations on why he didn't get any of the jobs. Some said he was overqualified for the position while others talked about how difficult it was to select from a pool of 'exceptionally well-qualified candidates who applied for the job'. He was most taken aback by the outcome of his sixth interview. The interview was in early February - just two months before his student visa was due to expire. If the visa were not renewed, he would have to leave the country immediately, for then he would have become an *illegal immigrant*.

He found he had received some letters when he returned from the Friday prayers. One was from Regina, greeting him from The Gambia. Yes, The Gambia! She had gone there to volunteer for a charity organisation. She also wanted to use the opportunity to know Africa a bit more. She said she was fine and was doing quite well and that The Gambians were fabulous.

Another envelope was from his university. It contained his Masters degree certificate. He held the certificate, admiring it for a while with satisfaction. "I did it!" he finally muttered to himself.

The white envelope that had a queen-figure stamp on it caught his attention. He deliberately kept it aside, preferring to finish with the other letters before returning to it. He wanted to read it last – as the concluding chapter of his joy that Friday evening. He had received his certificate and had received a nice letter from his beloved friend, Regina

At last he opened the letter in white A4 envelope, with the seal of the Crown. It read:

Dear Sir,

I write following the interview that we conducted with you on 12 January (??) in our central office for the post of Junior Development Analyst at our regional office in Dakar, Senegal. While we were impressed with your skills and qualifications, we have been advised, based on your published works that you sent to support your application, not to offer you the job. There are strong feelings that your political and ideological orientations, as reflected in those writings, may not allow you to be more understanding to our prioritisation strategies.

We thank you for your interest in the position and wish you good luck in your job search.

Sincerely yours

Elizabeth Cotton
Senior Personnel Manager

Samassi got very confused. He kept wondering what was wrong with the writings he submitted with his application. He had in any case never fully trusted these NGOs and had long concluded that they were more interested in getting publicity for themselves and jobs for young unemployed, barely skilled Westerners looking for adventure, international experience, and fun.

11

Samassi and Alex were very good friends. They were from different countries, practised different religions and studied different subjects. But they had similar visions of Africa, and often enjoyed discussions about the continent.

One day they had a very remarkable discussion about North Africa and sub-Saharan Africa. A few of their friends took part in the discussion, some of them non-Africans. Nigeria and Libya – both oil rich countries, were used as case studies.

"Is it the curse of the black man to be always the underdog?" Samassi had asked. There were many explanations for the apparent situation. One of the black Africans taking part in the discussion began a discussion about the slave trade and how it had left a certain mental reflex on black Africans. He blamed the Arabs for starting it all. Another talked about imperialism and neo-colonialism. One white girl blamed it all on corruption.

Samassi had a different explanation:

"Look at Nigeria and Libya", he began. "Slave trade and imperialism may explain some of the differences in their rate of development. But will it adequately explain why Nigerians, many of them highly educated, will have to go to Libya to do menial jobs while Libyans will never consider going to Nigeria to do menial jobs?"

He paused.

No one tried to interrupt him. They were apparently interested in that line of reasoning.

"The irony is that Nigerians are better educated people than they are and both countries have more or less the same quantity of natural resources. Sub-Saharan African countries are also generally less undemocratic than their North African neighbours."

Samassi continued: "We have to accept that the leaders of the Maghreb countries tend to be more visionary than their counterparts from sub-Saharan Africa." They all seemed to agree on this. Someone talked about Tunisia, and how the country was becoming increasingly a prime destination for many Western holidaymakers and sub-Saharan African students, especially those from the Francophone countries.

The belief that things could be different back home was one of the sources of strength for Samassi as he continued his job search. He didn't want to give up too easily because as he always said, a "quitter never wins, and a winner never quits." As his economic situation continued to deteriorate, he began applying for all sorts of jobs, hoping to find an interim job that would pay the bills while he continued with the job hunt.

One day he applied for a "warehouse operative" position, or so they called it. It was a nice title that, removed of political correctness meant that he got a job as a factory labourer.

Shortly after he began the job however, he became seriously ill. It was a hard and tough job, which physically drained him.

One of the recruitment policies of the company that owned the warehouse was that since some types of work demanded real physical strength and, thus, obvious fitness, the health status of all applicants had to be rigorously examined before any job offer could be made. Samassi had passed the interview, including the fitness test. But even if he really wasn't, the man who interviewed him would have offered him the job anyway. It was Easter and the warehouse was incredibly busy.

He had fallen ill in the presence of the Managing Director who had come from the company's head office to assess the work in their warehouse that night. He was a man who took the government's Health & Safety regulations at the workplace very seriously. He immediately asked to see the person who interviewed Samassi. They told him that the person who interviewed Samassi was attending a meeting.

He asked Samassi to take time off to recover and to see him in his office after his recovery.

While recuperating, Samassi was very concerned about the man who interviewed him. Why did the managing director want to see him? Was it obvious to him that he (Samassi) should not have been employed? He did not cherish the prospect of being the cause of the man losing his job. He knew the man who interviewed him had been working for the same company for fifteen years.

After his recuperation, he went to see Peter, the managing director, as instructed. He had a great sense of foreboding and was visibly nervous.

His secretary asked if he had an appointment with him, and when he said yes, he was told to wait in the secretary's office because the managing director was having a meeting.

When he was eventually ushered to the office, Peter had difficulty recognising him. He came, attired in his best suit and wore a new pair of black shoes that were so polished that one could see one's reflections on them.

Peter was about to ask him some questions when Jane, the secretary entered.

"Mr Dupont is here Sir. He is one and half hours too early".

Peter was visibly panicked. He quickly looked at his watch. "What about the interpreter? Is he here?"

"No sir, he is not due here until the next one hour ".

"Give him a call, if possible on his mobile. Ask him to take a cab immediately. Ask Mr Dupont in", he said, standing up to adjust his suit.

Mr. Dupont was a successful businessman from the French-speaking part of Belgium who owned his own company. He had been looking into the possibility of opening a branch in the UK with a local partner. They had been communicating in English in writing. Because Mr Dupont's spoken English was very basic, they had agreed to provide an interpreter when he visited.

Mr Dupont was ushered into the office. Samassi knew he should give them privacy but decided to wait for Mr Dupont to come in first.

The Belgian millionaire, a medium built man with funny eyes, entered, clutching a brief case. He shook hands with Peter, exchanged a few pleasantries with him in broken English and then turned to Samassi who was about to scurry out of the office.

"Bonjour monsieur", he said, shaking his hands, and mistaking him for the interpreter.

"Bonjour monsieur. Soyez le bienvenu," he replied confidently. They then began a long banter in French, with the Belgian asking him where he came from originally and telling him of his experiences in some of the African countries he had visited.

"Can we offer you anything? The interpreter is on the way. We weren't expecting you to be this early", Peter said. Samassi translated this into French for the Belgian.

The Belgian was taken aback, and so was Peter who looked obviously impressed with Samassi.

"He not the *intofretor*?" the Belgian asked in his brand of English.

"No, but he is our staff", Peter said with pride.

"But he *bery* good. *Excellenté* French", the Belgian said.

"May be you can help us out here. What's that your name again?", Peter asked, a very friendly smile on his face.

"Samassi".

******

Samassi became the interpreter and was very good at it. At the end of it all, Peter instructed that Samassi should be paid for the service, at the rate that was to be paid to the interpreter previously engaged.

Samassi was very happy. The money was handy. He got home and was about to open his door when his mobile phone rang. It was Peter, the managing director. He wanted to personally thank him for helping out as the interpreter. By the way he had a job for him. Yes, he knew of his immigration status but the company would help him sort it out.

12

In London, Samassi met many Africans. They had different reasons for being in the UK and had varying experiences of social exclusion, loneliness and homesickness. He also noted the disproportionately high number of black and other ethnic minorities who had mental health problems. He couldn't help wondering why. Could it be that living a minority existence is by definition stressful?

One day he went to one of the corner shops in Camberwell Green to buy vegetable oil. Asians – mainly Indians, Pakistanis and Sri Lankans, dominate these corner shops, normally called 'newsagents' or 'off-licences'.

It was late evening. The lady at the counter was an African – in fact a fellow West African. True, West Africans in London did not particularly feel any special bond among them. But the lady at the counter was different. She was in fact from the same country as Samassi and knew him rather well following an earlier encounter with him in the shop. Her 'off-licence' was one of the few owned by Africans. She co-owned the shop with her husband, an ageing Scottish man. Both worked in the shop.

They exchanged the usual pleasantries. Her husband, Mr Richardson, he was told, had travelled to Scotland and would be away for a few days.

He was among the last to be served that night. The Richardsons worked seven days a week – from 8am to 12 midnight, taking turns in the shop, sometimes with the help of two paid shop assistants. Samassi was there when she began locking up. They kept speaking in their native language about the situation in their home country and Samassi couldn't help pitying her when he learnt she had not been back to their country since she left some fifteen years back. She also said she had no contacts with her family.

"Where about do you live? If it is towards the direction of my home, I could give you a lift", she said after she had finished locking up the shops.

Samassi told him where he lived.

"That's fine. I will drop you off", she offered.

"That's very kind of you", he said.

As she entered the car, with Samassi sitting next to her, she mentioned of how hungry she was and how she couldn't wait to get home to "eat, take a hot bath and go to sleep".

"How can you be so hungry when you have been in the midst of food all day?" Samassi joked.

"I don't eat junk food. What you can buy in shops, as foods are junks. I eat healthy, real African foods", she said proudly and then told him of the local dish she had prepared the night before. Samassi said the dish was also his favourite but that he was conserving his appetite for the dish until he returned back to their home country.

"Why wait that long? You can come and have some. I live only a few blocks away. I can always drive you back to your home."

It was an offer he couldn't refuse. He didn't need any persuading before he eagerly accepted the offer.

The food was a mixture of red palm oil, cassava leaves and all the rest of it. Samassi felt immediately at home and thought of his mother who used to cook such food for him.

As they ate and 'washed the food down', she began to talk, first nostalgically about their home country, then about how horrible things have been for her in the UK and of her desire to "one day return home."

"But how come you haven't been home for so long? I know it is not easy running an off-licence. But you could take at least one week, once in two years, to visit home." Her countenance fell. Music – an old 1980s CD music from their country was being played, perhaps a little too loudly.

"It's more complicated than that."

Samassi said nothing, knowing that whatever it was must be a private matter. It was her decision if she trusted him enough to tell him whatever it was. She filled her glass with the red wine, crossed her legs and said: "Life could be tough".

"Oh I know that. I have been through hell here", Samassi said.

Later, after she had taken more of the red wine, she told Samassi how she met her Scottish husband. She was, she said, actually married to a very nice and caring man. One day she met Richardson, who was then visiting their country on a business trip. He had showered her with money and gifts. By the time she knew it, she was having a secret affair with him, behind her husband's back. He kept contacts with her after he returned to Scotland, sending her money and telling her how much he cared for her.

"I don't really think I loved him. It was more the money and the promise to help me and my family immigrate to the UK. I was naïve and young and stupid". She paused.

Samassi said nothing, and not knowing what to do, took a long sip from his glass of orange juice.

She moved from the sofa where she sat to where he sat. She drank another mouthful from her glass of red wine and continued.

"When he offered to invite me to live with him in Scotland, I couldn't resist. So one day I deliberately stirred a quarrel with my husband and then picked my things and said I was moving to my brother's who lived with his family in another quarter in town that was quite far from where we lived. Three days later I was with him in Scotland."

Samassi took another sip from his glass, scratched his head and said nothing.

"It is a decision I still regret to this day. My family felt I brought shame on them when they found out what happened and more or less disowned me. My parents were devout Muslims."

"They disowned you?"

"More than that. They called me a prostitute to my face and my husband's people would probably kill me for apparently nearly driving their son insane. He did not handle the situation well".

"Well, time heals every wound", Samassi said consolingly.

"I m not sure about that... or that I will ever be courageous enough to see any one that knew me."

"What does your husband think of the situation?"

"Oh, he is a pig. He keeps telling me to put it behind me or to stop whinging. Oh God, how I hate him!"

Samassi shifted uncomfortably where he sat in the sofa, trying to digest what he had heard without betraying his feelings.

"Are you married? Or you have girl friends? The questions jolted him back to the real world. She was holding his hand, caressing his palms and trying to appear sexy. He felt awkward and suddenly had a strong urge to visit the loo.

<u>13</u>

Samassi loved his new job. He was designated Public Relations Officer, though he was more of a Sales Rep especially to French-speaking countries. His ability with the French language was very much appreciated. A few months into the job, he was given a company car.

Back home, his mother's health continued to deteriorate. Samassi was very much saddened by the news. He wished she would live much longer, to see what he had made of himself in Europe. He had a good job and did a lot of travelling but he never forgot where he came from. He never forgot the misery of his student years.

As summer approached, he decided to spend the summer holiday back home. He was missing his mother so much.

As the Air France Boeing 747 began preparing to land at the airport in his home country, he looked down below to see what appeared to be a shattered town. The city, which he had held in such a high esteem before his travel, now looked like a remote village burnt down by bush fires. He swallowed hard. "What's going on here?" he muttered to himself

The plane landed safely, though with a big bang that jolted people in their seats and scared the faint-hearted. The plane taxied through the runway and then made an abrupt stop. The couple sitting next to Samassi, apparently Christians did a sign of the cross. The elderly man sitting just in front of him brought out his prayer beads. Samassi looked around. No one said anything but there was a suppressed sense of panic.

He looked through the window, trying to fathom out what was amiss. He saw nothing but darkness. It was raining heavily. He was in his mind thinking of the contrast: He had left Europe's summer a few hours ago to embrace a season of rainfall. Two climates. Two different worlds separated only by a few hours flight.

His train of thoughts was interrupted:

"Ladies and gentlemen, this is Captain Charles Ducart, your pilot, speaking. On behalf of my colleagues of the cabin crew, we are deeply sorry for this delay in your journey. Our late landing was due to difficulties in locating the landing ground. We now understand that there is a power failure here at the airport, which is also the reason why we are still in this position.

However, we've just been told that the airport authorities are looking into the possibility of bringing two vehicles here so that their flashlights could allow the four passengers that are getting off here to make their way through to the arrivals' terminal. There, some lamps and candles will be provided for lightening.

Once more again, we're deeply sorry for the delay and, to our four honourable passengers, we apologise for the inconvenience and wish you a very pleasant stay in the country .We look forward to serving you again."

A short while later, three people stood up. The sense of embarrassment on their faces couldn't be denied. A fourth man stood up at the far back of the plane, with a sarcastic smile on his face. He was a white Frenchman sent by his company in France to provide some technical engineering support to a group of local engineers. As he passed through the sitting passengers, he journeyed with his eyes here and there, looking for someone to speak to.

In the arrivals lounge, as announced by the pilot, a large empty bottle of mayonnaise stood in each of the four corners of the lounge. In each one was a big candle.

The airport officers clustered around one of their colleagues. The man was smiling broadly, in a happy triumphant sort of way. His colleagues were applauding. There was a certain sense of achievement in the air. One called the big officer around whom they clustered 'a genius'.

"In Europe this is enough to make you for life, to make real money for you. All you have to do is just patent the invention and *dosh* will be flowing your way until the end of time," one of the men standing said excitedly and with the authoritative air of someone who had been there and knew it all.

The man they clustered round had had the wonderful idea of bringing in the mayonnaise bottles to protect the candles. They had been struggling to lighten up the lounge. But each time they tried, an unfriendly wind would force its way through the door, the only entrance to the only lounge of the only international airport in the country, and blew away the candles.

Samassi walked past the men, his face lowered to the floor as he walked. He was glad he was home but disappointed at the type of welcome, if that could be called welcome, at the airport.

As he sat in the rickety taxi that was driving him home, the taxi driver, a jolly-looking fellow, tried his best to engage him in a conversation. Samassi didn't mean to be rude but he simply wasn't in the mood for a conversation. He was rather interested in the news, which was blaring from the car's radio. It lasted the better part of ten minutes, with almost each news item beginning with "Mr President has done this", Mr President is planning to do that".

Samassi felt sick to the stomach but said nothing.

"The President is trying his best. But he has bad advisers. And then he listens too much to people from his ethnic group and the foreigners that want to steal our wealth."

"Why didn't they mention the power failure in the news?", Samassi found himself asking, more to himself than to the taxi driver.

The taxi driver burst into a hilarious laughter as if Samassi had asked something stupid.

Samassi said nothing, suppressing his fury.

"Sir, it seems you have been away for a very long time. It is just a power failure, nothing serious. It was not as if someone died from it or as if the electricity will never be restored again. You have been away for too long sir?"

"No, but what has being away for too long got to do with it?"

"Sir, because this is Africa and not Europe. Power failure happens but it will be back. In the airport power failure never lasts long. Within three days, the power will be restored. Even before three days."

"Three days?"

The taxi driver burst into another round of hilarious laughter as if to ask whether Samassi was from the moon.

"Power failure is not the same as people dying. Before even electricity, our people were surviving well."

Samassi felt that continuing the discussion with the taxi driver would be a waste of his time.

His mother was very happy to see him. Samassi could not help shedding a few tears. She looked quite different from the agile woman he left behind for Europe a few years ago. She looked rather frail, aged and malnourished.

"Mother," he said, "I have missed you all these years"

She raised her hands towards the sky, and began a popular local song used to celebrate great events.

"Hei", she exclaimed. "I never knew I would ever see you again. Samassi! You really look very healthy and wealthy. I hope you haven't married a white woman?"

Throughout that night, Samassi had difficulty sleeping. He was worried about his mother and how frail she had become. He was terribly disturbed at the thought that his mother might be nearing the end of her earthly journey.

The following morning, he went to the Ministry of Finance, Planning and Foreign Investment. His company had advised him to explore the possibility of setting up a subsidiary of the company in that country. Samassi didn't want to see anyone else in the ministry but the Minister himself. He knew his country very well and the mentality of the people. He must dress impressively. That mattered a lot.

As he sat in the Minister's waiting room, he noticed dozens of well-dressed ladies – young and the not so young alike, walking to-and fro the corridors, some deliberately swerving their hips to heighten what they must have considered to be their sex appeal. Samassi wondered whether they all worked in that Ministry and if they did, why they were not in their offices.

He was eventually ushered into the Minister's office, some hours behind the time scheduled. This was despite the fact that his company had made the appointment months back. In the office, Samassi was shocked to see the Minister and others in the office excitedly watching an opera on a European TV channel.

The Minister said that he had seen the business plan and that it had been explained to him, as he was not a specialist in the field. He pressed the buzzer and spoke briefly on the line.

"He is on the way. He knows more about this. He should be party to the talks."

A few minutes later, a middle-aged bespectacled man in woollen suit entered and curtsied to the Minister.

"Take a seat", the Minister said, motioning him to a chair.

"Yes sir, Your Excellency", grovelled the man.

The Minister introduced the 'expert' to Samassi.

For the next ten minutes or so, Samassi tried his best to sell the idea of the company being licensed to set up a subsidiary, highlighting the numerous jobs that would be created. The Minister and the expert seemed to listen with rapt attention.

Suddenly a telephone call came to the office. The Minister's face beamed with smiles as he took the call. For the next five minutes he was on the line, chatting hilariously, oblivious of their presence, constantly saying, "No darling, you completely misunderstood the situation."

"This is a private call. We have to give the Honourable Minister privacy", said the expert, and patted Samassi on the shoulder.

He led the way and Samassi followed as they left the office to give the Minister some privacy. Once outside the office, the expert asked:

"You are a citizen of this country?"

"Of course", answered Samassi.

"And you are behaving that way to the Minister, speaking long grammar and all that?"

Samassi was genuinely confused.

"You didn't even bring any gifts to him. You think we should start jumping up about all this blah blah and brouhaha about jobs and all what not. You think he doesn't hear such a million times a day?"

Samassi looked at the man straight in the eyes and said nothing.

14

It was now three years since Samassi last visited his country. He had felt bitter at the way the trip ended, in particular at the way the Minister behaved. The company perhaps did not believe Samassi was to be blamed in any way for its failure to land the deal. If they did they did not say so to him. Nor did it affect his promotions in the company.

By the standards of black people in corporations in Europe he had done well. And by the standards of African immigrants who spoke English with a heavy 'African accent', he had done exceptionally well. But Samassi wanted to go home. And home for him was his country in Africa.

After the disastrous trip to secure Ministerial permission to open a subsidiary of BML Group Plc in his country, he had felt bitter, even betrayed. He almost blocked the country out of his consciousness for nearly a year, vowing never to go back. He had put a lot of energy to convince his bosses that a subsidiary of the company in his native country would be very viable. He had felt he was doing his bit for his country – securing for them, on a platter of gold, foreign investments. Perhaps he had taken too literally the numerous expensive advertisements on glossy magazines by the government of the country designed to woo foreign investors. He couldn't believe that when eventually his bosses acquiesced to his pressures, it was his own country that screwed him.

Samassi began taking a lot of interest in the discussions about returning home. His friends had different opinions. Some told him that with his experience and exposure, he would do well back home – especially if he entered politics. Others counselled caution.

To be sure it wasn't an easy decision for him. Would the fascination and the attractions of his job derail him from his ambitions of going back home to do his bit for his country? Should he quit his job and go home? If he quit, what future lay there for him? And if he stayed on, so what? He would keep his job and then so what?

He took his annual leave, and went to France. He met many of his friends, and with each friend he also discussed his plans. Again the responses he got were varied. But his mind was made up by the time he returned from the holidays.

When he told his bosses of his decision, they were all shocked, but wished him well.

15

Was he too idealistic and utopian or just too naive in his judgements? Was he too stubborn or just plain stupid? People could draw their own conclusions. For Samassi's mind was made up. He was returning home, back to Africa from whence he came.

He chose to live in neighbouring Senegal, at least for a while before returning to his own country.

As he made his way through to the arrivals' terminal at Dakar International Airport, he heard a rather violent noise somewhere in the lounge. He saw a group of people protesting and the police doing something that was quite different from what he would expect them to do in situations like that. They were trying to calm the protesters down. That was very remarkable to him. He became more curious and moved towards the crowd.

Some white police officers were among the crowd. He wondered what they were doing in Senegal and what the brouhaha was all about.

As he came closer to the crowd, he saw a man showing off his arms and his back to the crowd. Another man, who was held by the police, was trying to break free from them. There was a young lady, visibly furious, who was crying and shouting. She was, in a mixture of French and Wolof, swearing and cursing. There was a white lady, blood all over her body, being led to an ambulance by the police.

He worried that a sort of chaos was descending on the airport and feared for his safety. He decided to move away from the crowd and find his way out of the airport. But when he approached the exit door, he discovered that a strong contingent of the Senegalese armed forces, not the police this time round, had cordoned off the airport. He later learned that they did so in a bid to prevent the violence from spreading into the city.

Now with no hope of leaving the airport, Samassi was forced to keep observing the scene. At the entrance to the arrivals' terminal, just behind him, were the police struggling to prevent an angry mob of young people from forcing their way onto the tarmac. But outnumbered by the crowd, the police were overpowered, and the angry protesters, men and women alike, burst onto the tarmac. A short while later, it became a full-scale violence.

Suddenly there were wailing sirens from the Senegalese fire brigade. Not far from the crowd, a thick cloud of flame appeared stylish in its acrobatic displays in the air. A passenger jet had been set on fire. It was an Air France Boeing 747.

Samassi was both confused and frightened. He approached a man standing not far from where he was to find out what was amiss. The man started to reply, but he was so furious that he suddenly had to excuse himself to go and join another chaotic scene in another part of the terminal.

There was a policeman not far from where he was, but from his expressions, Samassi felt it would be a waste of time trying to find out what was really going on from him. Finally he found a lady who was willing to explain the situation to him. She explained that the man who was showing off his swollen arms and bruised back earlier on, and the one who was being held by the police, as well as the lady who was crying and shouting, were part of a group of eleven people who had been forcibly deported from France. They were all Senegalese nationals, save one Gambian man. They were handcuffed, beaten and incarcerated before being forced to board the plane that was now set on fire by the angry crowd.

The lady added that the French police raided the eleven deportees' homes in the middle of the night. Some, she explained, were arrested at their workplaces. The lady was visibly angry and obviously supported the action of the crowd, including the torching of the airplane.

"They were not even given any opportunity to take any of their personal belongings with them. All their money, all they laboured for just disappeared like that. Is that fair?"

She posed the question as if Samassi was part of the French police.

"That's not fair at all", Samassi replied.

"Even while in the airplane, they were still handcuffed like criminals. Even that lady who was crying. When she wanted to go to the toilet, a male police officer had to accompany her."

The lady was militant. Samassi could not help but admire her convictions. It was nice to know that despite everything people could still be as patriotic as that. He was tempted to ask whether they demanded explanations from the French police to know if it was just immigration violation or whether the deportees were also involved in other offences like robbery and drug pushing. He changed his mind, realising that any question, wrongly formulated under the circumstances, would land him in deep shit.

The lady was still speaking. Samassi noticed that she wasn't wearing any shoes. She had pulled off her shoes and had put them in a plastic bag she was carrying. For Samassi, that was an ominous sign.

"One of the deportees had been living in France for seven years and they still deported him. The police said they had no *'papiers'* in France, and so what? Did they have *'papiers'* when they came here several years ago and colonised us? Did they have *'papiers'* when they established colonial rule against our people's wish and stole everything we had? Now, just because these people want to work in France and help their families, they are handcuffed and

treated like criminals because of *'papiers'*.
That's not right and someone has to tell
them that."

"That's not right", Samassi affirmed.

"Even now, there are many French
nationals in Senegal who are in the country
illegally, as their residence permits have
long expired. But the government keeps
quiet about it. If they want to treat our
people like criminals because of *'papiers'*,
our government must retaliate and also
treat their people like common criminals."

Samassi felt very sorry for the poor
fellows. He deplored the way they were
treated and empathised with them.

As he made his way out of the airport,
he could not help wondering what the
incidents at the airport portended for his
return to Africa

Suddenly he began looking for his
briefcase. He remembered he had in his
hand while talking to the lady. Quickly he
dashed back to the arrivals' terminals but
there was nothing there. For the next ten
minutes or so, he was frantically and
desperately searching for it. The briefcase
contained most of his important documents,
including his academic certificates and the
only manuscript of a novel he was writing.

It also contained most of the cash he had on him.

17

Samassi rented a flat in central Dakar. He had remitted money to one of his friends who paid one for full year's rent for the flat.

He was also fortunate because he was well educated. He had applied for a teaching job in Senegal and had sent copies of his certificate to one of the Universities in Dakar. The head of the department had agreed in principle to offer him the position, but with his certificate lost, they could not immediately offer him the job as they had promised. They had to wait for certified copies of the lost certificate from his University in the UK.

He was uncomfortable the way the head of department treated the loss of his certificates and insisted on certified copies before he would be offered the job he had been promised. He decided not to put all his faith in them.

He began to look for job, contacting as many prospective employers as he could. His experiences with employers in Senegal were quite similar with his experiences in the UK in many ways. In the UK he had applied to more than one hundred jobs before he got any, in Senegal, he had applied to as many as he could find, or think of. The responses he got in Senegal were also similar to most of the replies he got in the UK. Like in the UK, his applications were either not answered at all or came with a polite apology, and of course, a regret that they could not offer him the job.

He noticed one crucial difference between the UK and Senegal for job hunting. In Senegal, there was never a certainty that the applications or CV ever got to the right people or right department that would assess applicants for any vacancy. Someone could 'sit on' an application or made sure, for one reason or another, that the application was never among those sent to the right people who were supposed to receive such applications.

Like in the UK, his perseverance and persistence eventually paid off. He got a job as a teacher in a secondary school. He wanted to hang onto that while looking for something better. He had also learnt to insist on submitting his application himself directly to the relevant person or department.

One day, after he had been teaching for three months, he decided to stop in the office of one of the international NGOs where he had submitted a job application through some 'friendly black brothers'. He wanted to ensure that the application was really submitted, and to find out why they never wrote him to acknowledge the receipt of the application.

As he got there, he saw a white man standing outside the office, smoking a cigarette. His instinct told him to approach the man and tell him about his job application that was never acknowledged. But just as he was walking towards the man, Kodjo, the 'friendly' Senegalese 'brother' who had been exceptionally nice, and had given him tips on how to survive in the country, and had promised to submit his application directly to the Director on his behalf, tried to intercept and distract him.

"Hi brother, how are you doing today? I have been really hoping that you will come around soon. I thought of you just this morning. What a coincidence". Kodjo was walking towards him. But it also seemed to Samassi that he deliberately wanted to ensure that he (Samassi) did not talk to the smoking white man.

Samassi greeted him perfunctorily and went straight to the white man.

"Yes Sir, how may I help you?" the man asked.

"Well, I submitted an application CV for a vacancy you advertised in a local newspaper. It's more than two months ago but I still haven't even received a letter acknowledging the receipt of the application."

"Do you mean you applied for the public relations officer's position that we advertised in *Walfajiri*?"

"Yes, sir."

"So what's your name?"

"Samassi."

"We received only three applications for that position and I can tell you there was no application from any Samassi. Did you use another name in the application?"

"No sir".

"It could be the post. You know how it is here."

"I submitted the application in person. Through the gentleman I greeted a while ago."

"Well.. well.. He probably forgot to hand over the application to me. We are in the process of re-advertising the job".

Samassi's heart skipped with joy.

"So what qualifications do you have?"

"I have a master's degree in Development Studies from a University in London. I have also worked for a major UK company, performing similar roles as in the job you advertised."

"That sounds interesting", the man said.

"Do you have a copy of your CV with you here or you could get it shortly?"

Samassi fished out his CV, which was printed on a nice, watermarked, yellow paper.

The manager read the CV with interest.

"So you are fluent in both English and Arabic?" The manager could barely conceal his excitement.

"Yes sir."

He told Samassi that he was very impressed with his CV and would discuss it with his colleagues. He asked him to come the following Monday to the office for an interview.

A few days before the interview however something happened, which changed the course of his life. He came back from school to find a locally stamped letter in front of his door. The letter had his father's name written out in full. That was quite unusual for he always abbreviated his father's name in all his correspondences.

The envelope was also unique. It was in fact an internal envelope of the company he worked for in London and also bore the company's logo. He had about five of them in his lost briefcase. With a shaking hand and a skipping heart, Samassi opened the envelope. The letter was written in French. Its English translation would be:

Dear Sir,

I'm sorry for the inconvenience I may have caused you. I'm the one who took your suitcase at the airport about four months ago. For long, I've been thinking about what to do about the documents. The documents suggest they must be important to the owner, and since I can't use them myself, I have decided to return them to you. Fortunately you had your address in it.

If you come to Sartre Boulevard by the telephone box at 22:30 on Thursday, you will get back your suitcase and your documents. But I

*must warn you about something. If you happen
to see me putting it there, never ever try to find
out who I am or where I'm going. That could be
fatal to you!*

See you there, and on time.

A sorrowful man in town.

Samassi read the letter over and over again.
He was happy he was going to get back his
documents. He went to see his friend,
M'Bengue, and told him about the letter.
M'Bengue, too, was glad he was going to
get back the briefcase.

They went to the designated area a few
days earlier to master its geography. He had
his suspicions but quickly brushed it aside.
The worst he expected was that the person
would ask for more money.

On the appointed day, he hired a taxi, and
asked his friend, to accompany him. They
explained to the taxi driver that they had
come to pick up a briefcase from someone
and that he should wait and drive them
back.

On their way, about half way from the
area, M'Bengue remembered that he had
forgotten to unplug the electric heater in his
rubber bucket at home. He excused himself
and hurried home, fearing the electric

heater might set his room on fire. They agreed to meet at Samassi's home once he had returned.

The taxi man didn't speak French properly and Samassi didn't speak Wolof at all. He was suspicious that Samassi spoke no Wolof, which almost everyone in Dakar spoke. He was even more suspicious when Samassi's friend suddenly changed his mind about the trip and dropped off. They didn't tell the taxi driver why he had to leave urgently. The taxi driver began to wonder: Whom are they meeting at this hour of the night in this isolated part of the city where there is no sufficient lighting? Are they part of the gang wanted by the police for the killing of Mr. N'Diaye, the owner of the big supermarket chain in town, two weeks ago, and thought to be responsible for the killing of two other people last week? He continued to drive, calmly, not saying much, amid these labyrinths of thoughts.

They got to the place earlier than agreed.

At around 22:23, they pulled on the roadside. They saw someone got off from the car, with something in his hand. The object seemed to him to be a briefcase. The person looked up and down the road. He then walked to an isolated and abandoned telephone box and pretended to be making a phone call. Seconds later, he returned to his car but didn't drive off.

Samassi excused the taxi driver and went to the abandoned telephone box. As he was returning with the briefcase, the parked car drove off. From his interior mirror, the taxi driver saw these. With a shaking hand, he hurriedly engaged the gear and sped off. He did not want to be linked to any crime. He had a wife and children to think of.

Samassi was confused. In desperation he began walking towards the city centre. After walking for about twenty minutes, he felt tired and decided to pop into the first bar that he came to. He ordered a drink and sat at a table, thinking. He didn't bother to open the suitcase.

Shortly after he entered the bar, the police surrounded the place. They were heavily armed.

"Stay where you are and put your hands up", one of the eight policemen ordered.

Silence descended on bar, with everyone looking around to find out who the police were after. Samassi was also looking around, trying to know who the culprit was.

"I say put your hands up now or I will shoot", one of the policemen who had a drooping moustache said, cocking and pointing his gun at Samassi. Samassi was surprised.

"Me?" he asked in surprise.

"This is the last warning. Your hands up or we will shoot".

Samassi raised his hands up. All eyes were on him. He looked distraught, not knowing what was going on.

"Stand up and walk away from that briefcase!"

Samassi did as he was commanded to do.

One of the policemen went to Samassi and frisked him for any weapons. Another took the briefcase and forced it open. He immediately called his colleagues to see the contents of the briefcase. It contained the equivalent of US$1,000 in CFA francs, a loaded pistol, and some of his personal documents, some of which bore his photo. There were also various documents in the briefcase, some with instructions on criminal operations being planned.

"We are arresting you for the murder of Mr. N'Diaye"

"Me?" Samassi asked in disbelief.

18

The three months that Samassi and his friend, M'Bengue, spent in the high security prison of Dakar were very difficult ones. They were often beaten up and deprived of food and sleep. They were treated as dangerous criminals. Most of Samassi and M'Bengue's friends however remained unconvinced that the two do anything criminal, not to talk of committing murder.

One of the reporters at *Walfajiri*, who knew Samassi rather well, was very convinced it was a set up. He was especially suspicious about the way the police arrested his friend, M'Bengue as an accomplice.

One day the reporter was in a taxi and overheard two passengers discussing the arrest of Samassi and his friend. Both appeared intellectual, with one mentioning that one of the two arrested had applied for a teaching job in their University a few months back. He mentioned how the man had claimed that his certificates had been lost and never showed up again when the head of department wisely insisted that he should produce a certified copy of the allegedly stolen certificate from his University in the UK.

The journalist politely interrupted them. He asked them if his details in the certificates he gave them were the same as the information about him and his qualifications published by the media. The men confirmed that they were exactly the same, with one saying he might have had other motives for the murder other than money. The journalist expressed his doubts.

Moussa had met Samassi a number of times. They had discussed about Samassi's experiences in the UK, hopes in Senegal and plans of eventually going to settle in his home country. He felt it was highly unlikely that Samassi was an armed robber. He couldn't imagine him being a murderer.

His editor, a left-leaning, fast-talking fellow gave him the permission to investigate. Moussa threw himself into the case with gusto. For the next two weeks, he spoke to as many people who knew Samassi as possible. He learnt of the day Samassi arrived Dakar, of the fracas at the airport at the time of his arrival. He also learnt that the office of Amnesty International in Dakar had filmed the scenes of the riots at the airport.

Moussa contacted Amnesty International and after two days of intense negotiations and exchanges of phone calls and faxes, it was arranged that Moussa and another senior editor would be given access to the tape 'but in the office of AI in Dakar'.

The amateur video recording of the incident by one of the staff of Amnesty International showed a footage of Samassi rushing to the rescue of a child who nearly fell on the floor from the back of his mother. Samassi was seen struggling to get the woman out of the crowd, and returning her child to her. He had placed his briefcase on the floor as he dashed to catch the baby from falling off her mother's back.

"This man! A criminal? I don't buy it", Moussa asked angrily and rhetorically.

"I don't too. Something is fishy", his colleague concurred.

"We have no judgement on this yet. It is our collective duty to find out the truth without being emotional. We are making our investigations and we can definitely work together on this matter", said one of the two Amnesty International's staff watching the

video with them. She was a small friendly
Senegalese woman, who was well-known
for her advocacy for human rights and her
fierce critiques of the practice of French
authorities of deporting people without due
course.

Walfajiri published the story a few days
later. It was a front-page story with the
caption: *Guilty as charged?* There were
photos of Samassi and his friend, M'Bengue,
beneath the caption. The story profiled
Samassi and his friend, including the
incidents at the airport the day he arrived
from the UK. The amateur video recording
of the incident was discussed in a separate
box, with an observation that the footage in
the video showed he had left the airport
without the briefcase. There was also
footage where he was frantically searching
for his briefcase. The readers were then
invited to arrive at their own conclusions on
whether they thought it likely that Samassi
and his friend could be behind the murder
of Mr. N'Diaye". A new angle was added to
the whole drama.

At the office of *Walfajiri*, the editor and
Moussa were planning the next strategy.
The papers had sold out within a few hours'
of coming out with the story. The editor

was happy and upbeat not just because the papers were sold out but more importantly because of the scoop. Phone calls were coming through to his office literally every second.

"The important thing is that a new angle has been added to the story. The next line is an investigation of the likely motives for the murder of Mr. N'Diaye. We have to look at his business dealings, talk to his associates, find out if he has conned any one recently, to talk to his wife. Raise questions about whether he was really killed by armed robbers, whether…"

Another phone call came through. The editor looked at the ringing phone briefly, as if he was deciding whether or not to pick it up. He answered the call.

"Oh yes," he answered, and for the next two minutes or so kept saying "that's right", to the person on the other end of the line.

"Moussa", said the editor, as if correcting the pronunciation of the name.

Moussa became alert.

"It's for you. Pan-African Association for Quality Journalism, Johannesburg ", the editor said, handing over the phone to Moussa.

Ordering this Book

*Wholesale inquiries for this book should be directed to any of the following:

Wholesale inquiries in the UK and Europe should be directed to one of the following:

Bertram, The Book Wholesaler:
+44 1603216 666: email: orders@bertrams.com

Gardners Books Ltd
+44 1323 521777: email: custcare@gardners.com

In the USA, wholesale inquiries should be directed to one of the following:
Ingram Book Company (ordering)
+1 800 937 8000 website: www.ingrambookgroup.com

Baker & Taylor (General and sales information)
+1-800-775-3700 Email: btinfo@btol.com

*Online Retail Distribution: www.amazon.co.uk,
www.amazon.com, www.barnesandnoble.com,
www.whsmith.co.uk, www.blackwell.com

*Shop Retail: Ask any good bookshop or
contact our office:
http//:www.Adonis-abbey.com
Phone: +44 (0) 20 7793 8893

Samassi

www.ingramcontent.com/pod-product-compliance
Lightning Source LLC
Chambersburg PA
CBHW031607260626
47154CB00020B/1704